FOR ALISON LOWE
WITH LOVE
~C.P.

FOR JULIA AND VICKY
WITH LOVE
~J.C.

LITTLE TIGER PRESS
An imprint of Magi Publications, London SW6 6AW
www.littletigerpress.com

First published in Great Britain 1998
This edition published 2003

Don't Be Afraid, Little One

CAROLINE PITCHER

ILLUSTRATED BY

JANE CHAPMAN

LITTLE TIGER PRESS

One moonlit night, while the wind
raged and the rain drummed on the stable
roof, a foal was born. His mother the mare
breathed on him softly, until he struggled
up on a tangle of long legs.

"What's that noise?" asked the foal. "Just the wind," answered the mare, nuzzling his velvety neck.
"Where is the wind?"
"It's blowing in the hills," replied his mother. "When you are big and your legs aren't wobbly anymore, you will run with the wind over the hills."
"Will you be there with me?" asked the foal.
"No," said his mother. "But you won't think of me then."

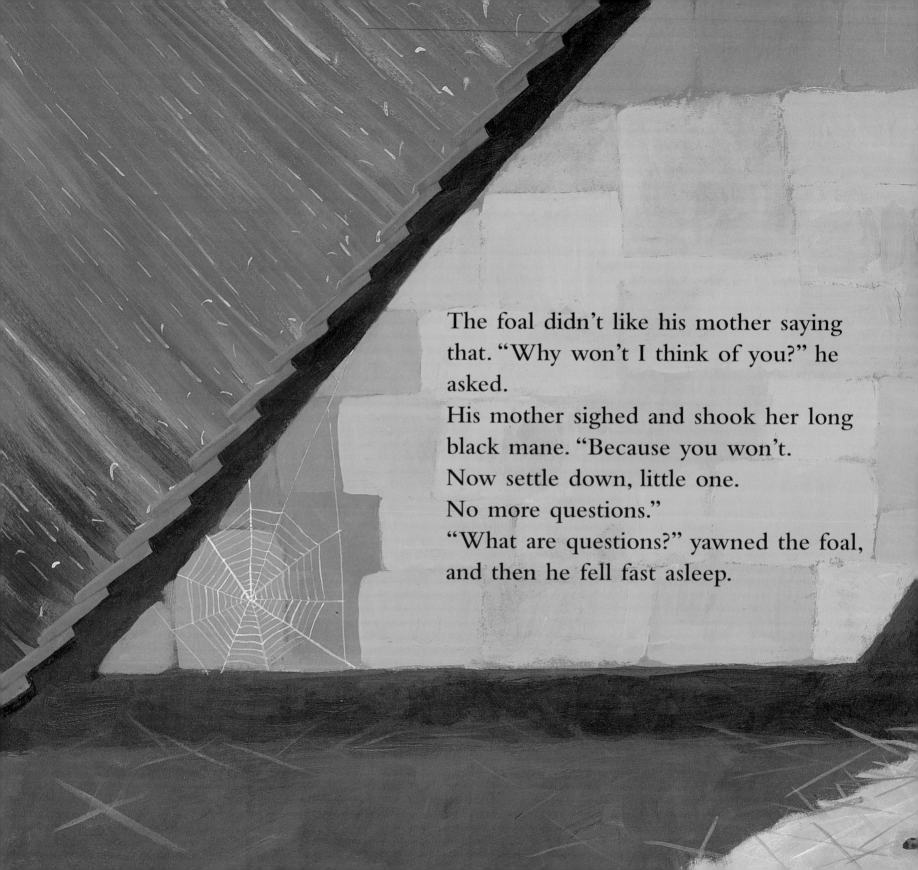

The foal didn't like his mother saying
that. "Why won't I think of you?" he
asked.
His mother sighed and shook her long
black mane. "Because you won't.
Now settle down, little one.
No more questions."
"What are questions?" yawned the foal,
and then he fell fast asleep.

Spring came, and the foal's legs
grew longer and stronger, so that
his head just reached the top of
the stable door.

"What's outside?" he asked.

"It's a field," said the mare. "Soon
you will be able to go there with
me and run all the way around
and back again."

"I don't think I want to," said
the foal, drawing back. "I don't
like Outside. I like it here."

The foal's legs grew even
stronger and longer. Now he
could see right over the stable
door. He saw other horses.
  There was a great shire horse with
giant hooves, and a tiny Shetland pony
with very long hair. He saw a horse as dark as
the night sky, and a pony as pale as moonlight.
"Where are their mothers?" he asked.
"Some of them are here and some are at
other stables," said the mare. "They give
people rides. I'll soon do that, too,
little one, while you stay behind."
Stay behind!

"No," said the foal, turning his back.
"I don't want to think about it."

When the days grew warmer,
the mare and her foal went out
into the field. They ran all the
way around it and back again.

Twilight fell, and the foal became uneasy.

"Can't we go back to the stable now?" he asked.

"No," said his mother. "When the nights are warm, we stay outside."

"But it's dark!"

"It's dark in the stable, too, little one. It's the same dark."

"It's not such a big dark there," said the foal.

"I can't see you out here when you move away from me. I'm all alone."

"You know I'm here, even if you can't see me," whispered the mare.

The foal lifted his head in the darkness.
"What's making that noise?" he asked.
"Just the wind. Don't you remember
hearing it when you were very small?"
"Yes," said the foal. "But where is it?"
"You know it's there, but you can't see it."
"Just like you in the dark, Mom," he
whispered.

One morning, the foal woke late. He
had done so much running and growing
the day before he was very tired. But
where was his mother? The foal looked
inside the stable, but she wasn't there.
Then he saw her by the fence. She had
a bridle over her head and a saddle on her back.
"I'm going back to work," she called
to him. "I'm going to give rides again."
"And who will ride me?" cried the
foal with excitement.
"You're too little to be ridden yet,"
explained his mother. "Your back is
weak, your mouth is soft as silk, and
your legs would snap like twigs."
"But I'll be all alone," he
wailed. "Oh, please stay
with me!"

"No," said the mare, as a little girl climbed
on to her back. "You'll be just fine."
The foal watched as his mother and her
rider trotted out of sight. He was all alone.
"Come back, Mom!" he neighed, and his
voice echoed in the hills.

He heard something answer
him, but it wasn't his mother.
It was the wind!
The wind had come down from the
hills to play with him. It blew in his
mane and his tail, and it blew in the
trees and stirred all the leaves. It blew
a butterfly for the foal to chase, and
it blew a path in the meadow that he
could run right through. It even blew
waves in the water of his
drinking trough.

The foal jumped and ran and
bucked and chased and flicked
his little black tail. He ran with
the wind all morning.

And then, just as the foal was too tired to run and jump anymore, his mother came back. She nuzzled his neck and said, "You see — nothing bad happened to you when you were alone."

Oh my, thought the foal. I was having so much fun I didn't think of Mom once.

"I wasn't alone," he said. "The wind played with me."

"So you didn't think of me at all?"

"Well, maybe a little bit," said the foal.

"That's good," said the mare. "I was thinking of you the whole time!"